MIRRORED IN MURDER

TRASH TO TREASURE COZY MYSTERIES, BOOK 3

DONNA CLANCY

SUMMER PRESCOTT BOOKS PUBLISHING

To the Cozy Community
Thank you for your continued support.

CHAPTER ONE

"I can't believe what you have done to this place in just a few short months," Sage said, plopping into the swivel chair to get her hair cut. "The addition Rory built on the back of the building gives you so much more room."

"I had to accept the fact I had outgrown the original floor plan. When I took on the three new stylists to keep up with customer appointments, it got really overcrowded in here with four stations and chairs. Luckily, Rory was in between jobs and took on building the addition for me."

Rory Nash was Gabby's fiancé. He ran his own construction company, which was how they met. Gabby's father had hired him to build his daughter a house and salon on the far side of the property he owned as a graduation present when she graduated from beauty school at the top of her class.

"Now I am wondering if the whole thing was a mistake," Gabby said, frowning.

"What are you talking about? Look how busy it is in here," Sage replied.

"I took out a small home equity loan against my house to build the addition, and now the new salon has opened at the center of town, and some of my customers have started to go there because they don't have to drive all the way out here."

"Have you lost many customers?"

"A few, but I'm afraid once bad weather returns, I'll lose a lot more. Many of my customers are older and don't like to drive in the snow."

"Don't get mad at the messenger, but my mom told me the salon owner is undercutting all your prices to steal your customers."

"Figures. That really irritates me because I have always tried to keep my prices at the lower end of what I could charge because of the income level in Cupston. And now she's undercutting me? That's really sad."

"Mom told me no one even knew she was going

to be opening a salon there. One day the building was empty, and then overnight, her business was there," Sage said.

"How much am I taking off today?" Gabby asked, poised with her shears in hand.

"Just the dead ends, please, and trim the bangs."

"Your hair is getting really long. The first time I cut it, it was above your shoulders, and now it's a little bit past your waist. Doesn't it get in the way when you're working in your shop?"

"It's always pinned up in a ponytail when I'm out there," Sage replied.

"It's such a pretty color," Gabby stated, combing out Sage's wet hair. "I wish my hair was naturally auburn like yours. No, I got stuck with boring brown hair."

"But you do such wonderful things with the highlights in your hair it looks anything but boring."

The phone rang, and Gabby had the closest chair to the reception desk. She answered the phone, and Sage could see her friend biting her lip. She hung up and slowly walked back to Sage after scribbling something out in her appointment book on the desk.

"What's up?"

"That was Hattie Perkins. She cancelled her

appointment for Friday because while she was at *Coffee Town* on Main Street this morning, the new salon owner came in and was handing out discount coupons for first-time visits. Hattie said she could save fifteen dollars by using her coupon and was going there instead."

"I hate to say it, but when you live on social security like Hattie does, fifteen bucks can buy a lot of groceries," Sage said. "She did say first-time. Maybe she'll come back after she uses the coupon."

"Can you do me a big favor?" Gabby asked.

"Sure, what do you need?"

"I want you to go to the new salon and poke around for me. Check her prices and see who she has working for her. I know she's offering manicures and pedicures, which I don't, and that's one service she has up on me, besides undercutting my prices."

"I don't want her touching my hair. You're the only one I let cut it," Sage replied.

"I'll give you the money to have your nails done," Gabby offered. "I really need someone on the inside to tell me about the place."

"I feel like I'm in a spy novel," Sage said. "Keep your money. I'll go get a pedicure. I've always wanted to try one but didn't want to drive to Moosehead to get it done."

"Thank you. I knew I could count on you," Gabby said, hugging her friend. "No charge for today's visit."

"You can't be doing that. You need all the paying customers you can get right now," Sage said.

"How's Smokey and Motorboat doing? They must be getting big."

"They are, and they are eating me out of house and home. I had to get one of those automatic feeders and fill it with dry food to keep them happy."

"I guess enough time has passed that it's a pretty sure thing they will be staying with you permanently?"

"Yeah, they're there to stay. I made appointments at the vet to get them fixed and all their shots. I'm going to get them chipped at the same time in case they get out on me and wander away from the house."

"Good idea," Gabby replied, cutting an inch off the back of her hair. "Speaking of houses, you know, we both have been pretty lucky thanks to our parents. Tomorrow is the anniversary of when I moved into my house."

"We have been extremely lucky," Sage agreed.

"Both of us were given our first house and will never have to worry about paying for a mortgage. We both had the ability to go into the business we chose to pursue. I had the freedom to get a home equity to add on here, and you have a massive workshop space right at your house."

"True. Cliff and I have been talking about screening in the back deck so the cats can go out there during the day while I'm out in the workshop. I don't want them to roam free outside because of the coyotes in the area, but I think they would like the fresh air of a screened-in deck. I wouldn't have the money to do that if I were paying a mortgage."

"Can you say spoiled?" Gabby asked, laughing.

"They are, but truthfully, I don't know if screening the deck in is more for the cats or Cliff. He hates mosquitoes, and we tend to sit out there a lot at night. Even the citronella candles can only do so much chasing the bugs away."

"It must be nice to have some peace and quiet back in your life after the ruckus with your cousin."

"It is but I feel bad for my mom. She has to go testify against him next month. She pretends it doesn't bother her, but I can hear it in her voice that it does. The one good thing that came out of it is my dad called my mom and told her he backed her one hundred percent in what she was going to do. It's the first thing they have agreed on since their divorce."

"There is another good thing. You got to keep

you-know-what," Gabby whispered, leaning in so no one else would hear her. "Did you get the diamonds appraised yet?"

"No, they are still hidden away in my safety-deposit box. And only a handful of people know about them, and they have been sworn to secrecy," Sage quietly replied. "I'm pretending they don't exist."

"Your mom was telling me she got you almost three thousand dollars for the diamond and pearl necklace that was among the jewelry you found in the unit."

"She was pretty happy because her cut was fifteen percent," Sage said, smiling. "I have to admit, my mom does know her jewelry and its value. There's a ruby and emerald ring that Mrs. Snow is interested in purchasing, but my mom wanted to get it profession-ally appraised first."

"I am pretty positive when I say you will never ever get another unit like that one again," Gabby said, spinning the chair around toward her. "Close your eyes so I can trim your bangs."

"And you were harassing me because I was spending too much money when I was bidding," Sage said, joking with her friend.

"Done. Do you want me to blow-dry it?"

"No, I think I'll let the wind do it on the way to my mom's shop," she replied, getting up from the chair. "Now, what do I owe you?"

"I don't know…"

"How much? You need paying customers right now. Someday when I'm seventy and have no money I'll take a free haircut," Sage said, smiling.

"Twenty dollars as it was just a wash and a trim," Gabby replied.

While Gabby rang up the sale in the register, Sage slipped a ten under the picture of her and Rory on her station. She knew her friend wouldn't take a tip, and this was the only way she could give her one and get out of the salon before Gabby realized it was there.

"I'll let you know how my appointment with the enemy goes," Sage said as she went out the door.

Pulling up to the front door at *This and That,* Sage opened the back doors to her van and started to unload her latest flips that her mother would sell on consignment. There were two sets of four dining room chairs. Sage had refinished the wood and reupholstered the seats: one set traditional and one more modern.

The battered dry sink had been refurbished into a classy bar, complete with a mirror that reflected the colors of the various liquor bottles when lined up in front of it and a double row of wine glass racks where eight glasses could be hung from each one. At the very bottom of the bar, Sage had inserted x-shaped wooden slats where wine bottles could be stored on their sides.

The two fire extinguishers had been cleaned up and polished. She had wired them and made them into two lamps and labeled them as industrial glam. The shades were grey in color which gave the set a sleek, finished vibe.

"Need any help?" her mom asked, coming out the front door.

"You can take the lamps in if you want," Sage said, crawling back into the van.

The last piece coming out was the largest and heaviest. Sage had taken one of the headboards and footboard that was in the storage unit and turned it into a hall entrance piece. She cut the footboard in half and attached each piece perpendicular to the headboard. Building a bench with storage space she slid the unit in between the two cut pieces of footboard and attached it. She finished the piece by painting the whole thing a dark tan and creating a cushioned seat covered in a material of tan, orange, and turquoise.

"I know who is going to love this piece," Sarah

said, getting on one end of the bench and helping to take it down from the van.

"Mrs. Fenster?" Sage, asked, smiling. "I was thinking of her when I designed the piece."

"I'm going to call her as soon as we're done," Sarah said.

Sage and her mom carried the piece into the shop. Flora was looking over the bar.

"Paul's birthday is coming up, and I think he would love this piece. He's turning one of the rooms in the house into a man cave, and I think this would be perfect for it," Flora said. "Put a sold sign on it, please."

"I guess I better get back home and keep working. All you have is the chairs and lamps left to sell," Sage said. "Maybe I need to crank out some smaller pieces to fill some spaces at the back of the shop."

"Sounds like a plan. Just don't show anything you make to Gabby, or the pieces will never make it here," Sarah, said, laughing.

"Speaking of Gabby, she is really down right now," Sage said, frowning.

"It's the new salon, isn't it?" her mother asked. "I knew that new owner was going to cause problems for our Gabby."

"She is giving away coupons all over town undercutting Gabby's prices. Her long-time customers are going to the new place because of the savings."

"What a shame. Gabby has worked so hard to build her clientele, and she just built that new addition."

"I had my appointment at Gabby's salon, and my hair looks wonderful. I already booked my next visit for three months from now for a touch-up," Flora said, running her fingers through her hair. "Do you like my pink streak? Gabby said it would make me feel younger, and it does. I love it."

"It does make you look trendy. I have a pedicure set up for tomorrow at the new place. I told Gabby I would go check it out for her," Sage said.

"So you're going to do some spying for her?" Flora asked.

"I did hear that most of the people working in her salon come from Moosehead and are not locals. The only one who you might know is Brenda Mann. She graduated the year behind you and is the manicurist there," Sarah said.

"Someone has to look out for Gabby. Where did this woman come from, and why did she pick Cupston to open her new salon? I know business can be competitive, but if all your stylists are from Moosehead why not open up there instead? There are so many questions that need to be answered."

"I'm sure you'll get to the bottom of it, knowing your persistence," Sarah replied.

"I don't even know the name of the place," Sage said. "I haven't been in downtown Cupston for a few months."

"The name is kind of morbid if you ask me," Flora piped up. "Who would call their place *To Dye For*? Even with the word play, d-i-e into d-y-e, it's still morbid."

"That is a strange name," Sage agreed.

"Just like the owner," Sarah mumbled.

"What's the owner's name?"

"Madame Talissa Hand."

"Madame?" Sage asked.

"I believe I was told that she thinks she is a gypsy princess. Someone even mentioned that she might be opening a palm and tarot card reading room in the back of the salon," Sarah said, shaking her head. "The renovations on the reading room have already started."

"I wasn't looking forward to going on my spy mission, but now it might turn out to be interesting. How old is this Madame Hand?"

"What do you think, Flora? Maybe late twenties early thirties?" Sarah asked.

"I think so. She can't be much older than that."

"Wish me luck. I guess I'll head back to the shop and get some more work done."

"Let us know what you find out," Sarah said. "Now go home and get busy and bring me some more good stuff to sell."

Once in her workshop, she settled on her next project being a coffee table made out of a rustic lobster pot. Sage had been sitting on the piece for almost a year and had done nothing with it. It was time to fix and flip it. She ripped out the netting from the inside of the trap. Fighting with the urge to sand the whole trap down, she sanded only the really rough patches and left the rest as is. The first coat of polyurethane was added. While it dried, she cut a piece of glass that would be set into the top of the piece.

Moving on to a bedroom vanity, she took it out to the driveway to sand the piece, not wanting the dust to get into the fresh coat of polyurethane on the trap. Concentrating on removing as much of the old paint as she could, she didn't notice someone walking up behind her.

"Brenda! How long have you been standing there?" Sage asked, shutting off the electric sander.

"I need to talk to you," she replied, looking around the area nervously.

"Come into my workshop," Sage said.

Brenda Mann was the new manicurist at the shop Sage was going to investigate the following day. She had been the class president all four years of high school, and Sage had never known her to be a skittish kind of person. Something was wrong.

"Have a seat," Sage said, brushing off a bench for Brenda to sit down. "What's up?"

"I didn't know who else to come to," she started. "I didn't want to go to the sheriff because he'd probably think I was crazy and overreacting."

"Overreacting about what?"

"There is something going on at the new salon. Something that doesn't have anything to do with cutting hair or manicures."

"What is it?" Sage asked, pulling up a chair.

"That's the problem. I don't know exactly what it is, but I am sure it has to do with that back room they are renovating," Brenda replied. "No one is allowed back there besides Madame Hand or her husband."

"That is strange, unless they are doing it for safety reasons."

"It could be, but I have seen customers walk back there by accident looking for the bathroom, and she goes into a tither about it. And there is something else really strange."

"What?"

"Madame Hand is not a stylist. She knows nothing about any aspect of working in a salon. She's not a manicurist or pedicurist either. Why would you open a salon if you can't work in it?"

"Interesting."

"I don't know, maybe I'm overreacting, but nothing makes any sense about the place. And she is bad-mouthing Gabby all over town which infuriates me. I even threatened to quit if she didn't stop doing it, and she told me manicurists were a dime a dozen, and if I didn't like the way she ran HER salon, to leave right then and there."

"Not much of a people person, is she?" Sage asked. "Why don't you leave here and go talk to Gabby. She has room now for a manicure station and might hire you so you can leave the other place. She's wanted to offer your service for a while now."

"Really? I would quit with no notice if I could work for Gabby."

"Are you working tomorrow?"

"I am, but if I talk to Gabby and she offers me a

job, I will go, pack up my stuff, and quit the other place this afternoon."

"I'm going in there tomorrow to do a little checking out of the place on my own. I'm getting a pedicure which I have never done before."

"Steph does the pedicures, and you will love her, if she's still there. When I left today, Madame Hand was screaming at her for something. I don't even know if she'll be there for your appointment. Everyone is pretty fed up with Madame Hand at this point."

"It doesn't sound like she'll be in business too long," Sage said.

"The funny part is I don't think she cares. People quit, and she doesn't replace them, and the way she yells at customers, I'm pretty sure they won't return either."

"Thank you for the heads-up. I may have to accidentally on purpose walk into the so-called back room tomorrow during my visit to see what happens. If you are still working there, pretend you don't know me. I don't want Madame Hand's guard to be up."

"Thanks for listening. I'm going to talk to Gabby right now," Brenda said, standing up.

"Good luck. If I don't see you there tomorrow, I'll know you have a new and better job," Sage said.

"Be careful. Madame Hand is off the wall, and her husband is a very scary man. His coal-black eyes burn a hole right through you. Thanks again," Brenda said, heading for her car.

"Looks like tomorrow's visit to the new salon is going to prove very interesting," Sage said, watching Brenda drive away.

She finished sanding the vanity and then wiped it down with a wood cleaner to remove all the remaining dust. It was getting late, and Cliff was due in an hour for supper. She moved the vanity back into the workshop and locked the building up.

Half an hour later she had showered, fed the cats, and was starting to cook supper. There was a sale on swordfish at the local market, and she had stopped on the way home to pick a couple of slabs of fish up to cook on the grill.

Taking out a large piece of heavy-duty tin foil, she laid some butter and lemon slices in the bottom and then the two pieces of fish. Another layer of lemon slices, some dried sage, and salt and pepper were placed on top of the swordfish. Sage tightly closed the foil so that none of the juices would leak out. Setting the propane grill on medium, she placed the foiled fish on the rack and closed the top of the grill.

A fresh green salad sounds good, and maybe I'll throw some French fries in the oven.

Sage turned the fish twice before removing it from the grill. She was just setting everything on the table when Cliff pulled in. Waving out the kitchen window, she watched him go to the back of his truck and pull out a long roll of screen that would be used on the deck. He came through the back slider after laying the roll on the deck.

"I thought we were going to the hardware store on the weekend to get what we needed for the deck," Sage said as he washed his hands at the kitchen sink.

"We still need to go, but this was brought in as a donation for the fall farm sale. So I scooped it up and put forty dollars in the safe to purchase it for your deck."

"Wouldn't it cost a lot more than forty dollars at the hardware store?" she asked.

"It would, but you know yourself we always mark items down for the sale so everything will move. I think forty is more than reasonable, and it's what we would have charged had it been included in the sale."

"Okay, I just don't want the farm to lose money," Sage said, grabbing two beers from the fridge.

"Believe me when I say I would be the last one that would want the farm to lose money. Mom and

Dad have worked way too hard to keep the place going," Cliff said. "I have some produce in the truck for you. The second crop of corn is ready, and it is sweet and tasty. We can't keep it in the farm stand."

"We can have it tomorrow night. Gabby and Rory are coming over for supper."

"What's the occasion?" Cliff asked, digging into the salad.

"Nothing special. I'm going on a spy mission for Gabby tomorrow, and they're coming over tomorrow night to get the results," Sage said.

"A spy mission?"

Sage explained what was happening between the two salons and how Madame Hand was undercutting and bad-mouthing Gabby. Sage was going to find out more about the owner and her new business, nothing more. Cliff insisted she call him when she left the salon, especially after what he heard about the husband.

After supper, the couple retired to the deck and spent a little time snuggling together in the hammock until the mosquitoes got so bad neither of them could stand it outside anymore. Cliff promised to have the deck screened in by the coming weekend as he left for the evening.

Sage got into bed with the two cats. Crawling up

on the pillow next to her head, Smokey's tail kept swishing across Sage's face. After the fourth time, she moved the cats to the end of the bed. They stayed where they were put, and everyone fell asleep.

CHAPTER TWO

Sage was woken up the next morning by Motorboat dropping a catnip mouse on her face and then batting it around on the pillow next to her head.

"Okay, I'm awake already," she said, rolling over toward the edge of the bed.

Smokey sat at the foot of the bed patiently waiting for his owner to get up and serve them breakfast. He meowed several times as if saying good morning to Sage and then rubbed up against her purring.

"Motorboat, why can't you be more like your brother and not so pushy in the morning?" Sage asked the cat who was sitting on her pillow holding the toy in his mouth. "Come on, I'll get you guys some breakfast and then take my shower."

The cats each got a plate of wet food and ate

while Sage turned on her coffee maker. When she came out of the bedroom, the cats had finished their breakfast and were sitting in the bay window cleaning themselves.

Sage grabbed a cup of coffee and sat at the kitchen table reading through the classifieds for estate and yard sales. She circled the ones she was interested in going to with a red marker.

I love being in business for myself. I can set my own schedule and do things like going to yard sales or whatever else I feel needs to be done.

Because the cats woke her up early, she was able to add a second coat of polyurethane on the lobster trap and a base coat of primer on the vanity before she left for her appointment. Her mom had left a message on her phone that Mrs. Fenster loved the hallway piece and wanted to know if Sage could create a set of six dining chairs using the same material as on the bench. When she returned home, she would have to go out to her storage trailer to see if she had six matching chairs.

"You guys be good. I'll be home in a few hours," she said to the cats who totally ignored her as she went out the door.

After a quick stop at *This and That* to pick up her monthly consignment check, she drove into town for her appointment at the salon. Wearing a light cotton dress and flipflops, she was dressed and ready for her pedicure.

To Dye For was a salon looking like it could have been open back in the nineties. Sage could see the furniture had already been used when bought and the floor and walls had been untouched from the previous business that had been in there. A large sheet of cloudy plastic hung at the back of the main room concealing what was being done in the rear of the building.

I definitely have to check that out.

"How can I help you today?" a woman in a flowery, flowing skirt, white gauze blouse, and a bright purple scarf tied tightly around her long red hair asked as she approached Sage. "I am Madame Hand, and this is my salon."

"My name is Sage Fletcher, and I have an appointment for a pedicure at ten o'clock."

Madame frowned when she heard Sage's name.

"Wait here, and I'll see if Stephanie is ready for you," she said, strutting away, her huge, layered earrings clinking as she walked.

Boy, is she playing the part.

Loud yelling erupted from the other room. Two women were arguing, and their voices grew louder with each sentence spoken. The arguing came to a sudden stop when a woman about Sage's age came tearing out of the back room. She ripped her apron off and threw it in the face of Madame Hand who had followed her still screaming.

"If you walk out that door, don't come crawling back for your job," Madame yelled, throwing the apron to the floor after peeling it away from her face.

"I wouldn't come back here if it was the last job on the planet," the young woman screamed. "You're a lunatic."

The other customers and stylists were sitting there in stunned silence. The place was so quiet you could have heard a bobby pin hit the floor.

"I am so sorry," Madame said, clapping her hands. "Back to work ladies unless you want to be unemployed like Miss Stephanie now is."

"Um, excuse me. Was that my pedicurist who just went out the door?" Sage asked, already knowing the answer but wanting to play dumb.

"I am so sorry, but yes it was, and unfortunately, there is no other. I can give you a coupon for a free haircut to make up for your missed appointment," Madame offered.

"Don't take it," another customer whispered to Sage on her way out the door.

"I already have a hairdresser, thank you and I don't need the coupon," Sage replied.

"I know who you are. You are Gabby's friend. Did she send you here to spy on me?" Madame asked, her face turning red and her voice going up an octave.

"I am Gabby's friend, her best friend. She didn't send me here to spy on you. I've never had a pedicure, and you offered that service. Now it looks like you won't be offering that service either. I noticed your manicurist is not at work today. Did she quit too?"

"How did you know that?" she asked, eyeing Sage suspiciously.

"This is a small town and news travels fast. I guess you should have looked into things like that before you opened your business here," Sage replied.

"I guess I should have," Madame snarled. "And now you can find your own way out as I have to help the customer my useless clerk walked out on."

Madame disappeared into the back room. Sage could hear her apologizing repeatedly to the abandoned customer. Thinking this was the best chance she had to check out what was hidden behind the plastic curtain, she headed straight for it and slipped inside.

The walls had been stripped down to the two by

fours and the floor down to the plywood. Wires were hanging from the ceiling, and other than chalk marks drawn on the floor, the room looked just like a room that was being renovated.

So why are you being so secretive about this space?

"What are you doing in here?" Madame Hand screamed, planting her hands on her hips.

"I'm sorry. I was looking for the bathroom. I had two cups of coffee this morning, and they are catching up to me," Sage said, staring her down. "I needed to use the facilities before my drive home."

"The bathrooms are clearly marked out in the main room," she replied. "You are here to spy on me. I knew it! Ricardo!"

A six-foot tall man with coal-black eyes appeared at the curtain. He folded his arms across his chest and glared at Sage.

"Escort this person out," Madame said, grabbing Sage's arm as she started to walk by her. "And if you know what's good for you, you will never come back here again."

"And if you know what's good for you, you'll get your hand off my arm or you will never style another head of hair again," Sage warned her, showing no fear. "Bodyguard or no bodyguard."

"Get out!" Madame screamed at the top of her lungs.

All eyes were on Sage as she calmly and slowly walked out the door under the careful eye of Ricardo who was making sure she left the building. She got in her van and let out a huge breath.

Man, that guy is scary just like Brenda said. They are definitely hiding something, but what? It's going to be hard to figure out what it is now that I can't go back in there.

Stephanie was sitting on a bench on the opposite side of the street. She appeared to be crying, so Sage went to see if she could calm the poor woman down. She plopped on the bench next to her and smiled when Stephanie looked up.

"You okay?" Sage asked.

"Yeah, I guess so. That woman infuriates me, and I couldn't take her verbal abuse anymore. I'm sorry about your cancelled appointment. Brenda was so lucky to land a job with Gabby and escape the clutches of Madame Hand."

"You know about her new job?"

"Brenda called me last night and told me you sent her over to talk to Gabby. Do you think she might want to offer pedicures at her salon, too?"

"I can't answer that, but it couldn't hurt to go

ask," Sage replied. "I have a feeling this place isn't going to be in business too much longer, and it might be to Gabby's benefit to offer full service. I'm not saying she will say yes, but you never know. Can I ask you a question?"

"Sure."

"Did you notice anything weird going on in the room behind the plastic?"

"No, I can't for the life of me figure out why they were so protective of that area. I never saw them work in the room during the day, but when I would come to work in the morning you could tell they had been in there working at night," Stephanie replied.

"Is it true Madame Hand is turning the room into a palm and tarot card reading space?"

"That's the story, but I don't know if it's true or not."

"Thanks for answering my questions. Now go see Gabby and good luck."

"I'm going to go there right now and talk to her," Stephanie said, perking up and smiling. "Thank you."

Sage watched Stephanie walk to her car. She knew Madame Hand had been watching them from the door of her shop and didn't look happy when Stephanie climbed in her car and drove off.

"I bet Madame Hand was figuring Stephanie

would come back begging for her job, and it didn't happen," Sage said to the pigeon who had waddled up next to her foot looking for something to eat. "Sorry, I don't have a thing to give you. Next time, I promise."

While she was in town, she stopped at the bank and deposited the check her mom had given her earlier that morning. Sage was going to go to see Gabby but figured between clients and Stephanie popping in at the salon, her friend would be too busy to sit and talk.

A short time later, Sage was in her workshop applying a third coat of polyurethane on the lobster trap coffee table. She painted a quick drying base coat, lavender in color, on the vanity.

I need a bench to go with the vanity. I'll look for one and check for the chairs at the same time.

Rummaging through the storage trailer, she dug out a dainty bench she'd bought at a yard sale the previous summer. It would need a matching coat of paint to the vanity and a new cushioned seat added on the top. She could only find two sets of chairs that had four chairs not six like she needed. Carrying the bench in one hand and two shutters in the other hand she was going to turn into a storage unit, she slowly made her way back to her shop.

The afternoon flew by, and Sage had accomplished a good day's worth of work. She showered and started to prepare supper. Sitting on the deck husking the corn that Cliff had brought from the farm the previous night, she heard sirens in the distance.

"Something's going on in town," she said to Smokey through the screen door.

The chicken had been cooking on the grill at a medium heat for a good hour. Sage brushed the barbecue sauce she made herself out of ketchup, mustard, and maple syrup onto one side of the chicken before flipping it to coat the other side.

That smells heavenly.

Cliff's truck pulled into the driveway. He joined her out on the deck after he grabbed a beer from the fridge.

"I don't know if Gabby will be here anytime soon," he said, plopping in the hammock.

"Why? What's up/'

"Apparently, Madame Hand found out Gabby hired both Brenda and Stephanie. She went to Gabby's salon to confront her about stealing her employees," Cliff answered.

"I would have loved to be a fly on the wall for that," Sage replied. "Gabby was so mad about her name being slandered all over town she would have stood up to Madame Hand and told her off big time."

"I guess it got pretty intense according to my mom. She was there having her hair done."

"I'm glad Gabby hired both Brenda and Stephanie. She has room with the addition, and now people will have the option of going there instead of all the way to Moosehead. And they provide their own equipment and supplies so there is no additional cost to Gabby."

"Does Gabby get paid anything for having them in her salon?"

"She receives a small fee per customer. Kind of like when my mom receives a percentage of what I sell in her shop," Sage answered. "Plus, it might draw in more hair clients for her."

"I wonder if Madame Hand will let them remove their items from her shop or if she will try to keep their things," Cliff said.

"Knowing that lunatic, Brenda and Stephanie might have to have the law accompany them to the shop."

"Lunatic was the exact word my mom used when she described her," Cliff said, chuckling.

"I can't wait for Gabby to get here so I can hear her side of what happened," Sage said, opening the lid to the grill. "Speaking of, they should have been here by now. I'm going to take the chicken off the grill, so it doesn't get dried out."

"They just pulled in," Cliff said. "Wait a sec, it's only Rory."

They walked to the driveway to find out where Gabby was as Rory exited his truck looking extremely upset.

"Where's Gabby?" Sage asked.

"She's at the Cupston police station being questioned for the murder of Madame Hand."

CHAPTER THREE

"Excuse me? What do you mean she's being questioned?" Sage asked in disbelief. "And Madame Hand is dead?"

"Gabby closed the salon at four and went into town to pick up something for dessert for tonight. While she was there, she did some other shopping and was away from her house for a couple of hours. When she returned home, there were cruisers all around her salon."

"Am I to assume Madame Hand was in the salon?" Cliff asked. "A dead Madame Hand?"

"You got it. Someone anonymously phoned the police to say the body was there, and they overheard a fight between the two women. The caller said Gabby threatened to kill her."

"How convenient that it was anonymous," Sage replied, frowning. "How did they get into the salon?"

"Sheriff White told me in confidence that it appeared someone had tampered with the lock on the rear entrance to the salon. He believes the body was placed there to frame Gabby," Rory replied. "But he had to bring her in for questioning even though he doesn't believe she did it."

"Gabby must be a wreck," Sage said.

"She is. And the fight they had at the salon earlier in the day doesn't help Gabby's plea of innocence," Rory added. "She threatened Madame Hand that she had better stop slandering her name or else Gabby would make her stop."

"And of course anyone in the salon at the time heard Gabby say what she said," Cliff said.

"The salon was full at the time," Rory said.

"It does sound bad," Sage said. "Anyone that doesn't know Gabby like we do is going to think the worst."

"She meant she would sue her for defamation, not kill her," Rory said. "I was in the process of finding an attorney to hire."

"How did Madame Hand die?" Sage asked.

"I don't know. The police aren't releasing that information."

"Standard procedure. Is Gabby coming home tonight?" Sage asked.

"She's going to call me when the interview is done," Rory replied as they walked back to the deck. "Sheriff White wouldn't let me stay in the waiting room until she was done. He didn't know how long it would take."

"I wonder what will happen to the salon now," Sage said, turning off the propane grill. "Brenda told me Madame Hand didn't do anything but run the place. She couldn't even style or cut hair."

"And from the talk around town, the stylists she has working there aren't very good at their jobs either," Cliff added.

"I said from the very beginning that the salon was a cover for something else. No one would put money into a business and run it like they do. It has to do with that closed off back room. Something is going on in there, but I didn't have enough time to really look at anything before Madame Hand caught me nosing around and threw me out of the building."

"What did you see?" Cliff asked, handing Rory a beer.

"The room was stripped down to the basics, no walls and a plywood floor. The only weird thing was there were chalk marks on the floor in different areas of the room. Rory, as a builder, do you use chalk marks?"

"I do for several reasons. They could be marking the placement of future interior walls, where new pipes for plumbing are going to run under the floor or other utilities like electrical wiring."

"So I guess the chalk marks are nothing special either," Sage said, sighing. "I still have a gut feeling something is going on in the back room."

"Don't they have to have a building permit for what they're doing?" Cliff asked.

"Yes, they do. I can go to the town hall tomorrow and see what they pulled a permit for. As a builder, they wouldn't think anything about me asking," Rory replied.

"I don't think that's a good idea. Word will have traveled around town that Gabby is being questioned about the murder, and people might think you are trying to help her cover up something."

"Sage is right. I'd stay clear of anything to do with the whole situation," Cliff said, agreeing with his girlfriend. "You don't want your construction business to be called into question in the fallout."

"I need to be there for Gabby and do whatever I can to help though."

"You will be," Sage said, giving him a hug. "Let's

eat while we wait for that call. I'll put together a plate that you can bring home for Gabby to eat when she's done at the sheriff's."

"Sounds good. I haven't eaten all day," Rory said, sitting down at the picnic table.

Two bites in, Rory's cell phone rang. He told Gabby he would be right there to get her. Sage packed up two plates of food and gave them to her friend. She told Rory to give Gabby the message she would be over in the morning to talk to her.

"What a mess," Sage said, watching Rory drive away.

"It is, but I'm sure it will be straightened out, and Gabby will be cleared," Cliff said.

"She will be if I have my way," Sage declared.

"Don't you go messing around with the big guy with the black eyes at the salon," Cliff said, warning her. "Give it a little time to see if the salon even stays open."

"But what if they've finished what they were going to do and all of a sudden disappear? Gabby will never be cleared of the murder."

"Let the sheriff handle it," Cliff replied.

"I think I'll go see the sheriff in the morning before I go to Gabby's house. The salon will probably be closed for a few days as it's a crime scene. I feel so bad for her since the salon was pulling in new business every day and now she was going to be a full-service salon with a pedicurist and manicurist."

"Life is always throwing us curveballs," Cliff replied.

"I know. It's just not fair. She's worked so hard to build her business."

"She'll bounce back. Gabby is not one to give up."

"Our supper is stone cold, and it looks like the bugs have found it. Let's make new plates from the food in the kitchen and eat at the table inside," Sage suggested.

"Yeah, I'd rather eat food than be the food," Cliff said, swatting at the mosquitoes buzzing around his head.

As they ate, the conversation turned to the donations for the fall farm sale which had already been received. Sage asked if there was any furniture donated yet and in particular dining room sets. Cliff said one had come in consisting of a large table and eight chairs. She explained she had a customer request for a set with six chairs but didn't have the items in her inventory. He said he would ask his parents about the price and get back to her about it.

Cliff left a little before ten, and Sage was in bed

shortly afterwards. She didn't sleep much, tossing and turning, worrying about her friend. Even the cats couldn't take the constant movement and made their way down to the floor to get some shut-eye.

At sunup, Sage was busy out in her workshop. The final coat of polyurethane was applied to the lobster trap, the vanity received a coat of lavender paint, the seat of the vanity bench had been removed for reupholstering, and a coat of primer had been applied to the wood. At nine o'clock, she locked up and left for the sheriff's office.

At the front desk, Sage requested to speak to the sheriff. Deputy Durst called to see if he was available. He was and agreed to see Sage.

"I know my way to the office," she said to the deputy.

"Yes, you do," he replied, smiling and returning to the paperwork in front of him.

"Good morning, Sheriff White."

"Hello. I figured I'd be hearing from you this morning. Have a seat."

"Anything new on Madame Hand's murder?"

"No, we're working on it. It hasn't even been twenty-four hours yet. Cut me some slack."

"How did she die?" Sage asked.

"We don't know yet. There were no visible marks

present on the body to suggest a means of death. You do realize I shouldn't be discussing this with you?"

"I know, and I do appreciate the fact you have enough trust in me to do so. Please tell me you don't think Gabby did this."

"No, I don't think so, but I can't show favoritism. She has to be on the suspect list because of the threats she made, and the body was found in her salon."

"How did they get the body into her salon?" Sage asked, pretending Rory hadn't told her.

"Someone jimmied the lock on the back door of the salon."

"Where was the body found?" Sage asked.

"Here are the crime scene photos. I'm showing you these under the strictest of confidence. We haven't released any of this information to the public."

"I understand. How strange. This is how the body was left?"

"Yea, whoever dumped the body posed Madame Hand in front of a mirror."

"They didn't waste too much time in the salon. The body is in the chair closest to the back door. Whoever did this, didn't know how long Gabby would be away and wanted to get in and out in a hurry."

"My thoughts exactly."

"Sheriff, the coroner's results are here for the Madame Hand autopsy. He put a rush on it," Deputy Durst said, handing the sheriff a folder.

The sheriff opened it and glanced over the contents.

"Interesting," he mumbled.

"What?"

"It seems our victim was not murdered. She died of a brain aneurism. The coroner has ruled it to be a death by natural causes, not homicide."

"Why on earth would someone take a body that died of natural causes and put it in Gabby's salon?"

"Revenge?" the sheriff replied.

"This gets stranger by the minute. What is Madame Hand holding in the photo?" Sage asked. "It's not very clear."

"I'm not sure. I'll have to find out what was removed from her hand from the crime team."

"In my opinion, take it for what it's worth, this whole thing revolves around the new salon and what is hidden in the back room there. I believe two of Madame Hand's employees were going to start working for Gabby, and someone at the new salon might have been afraid they saw something in their short time working there. Maybe by putting the body at Gabby's place, they figured it would keep the salon closed and the new employees couldn't talk to anyone about what they saw at *To Dye For*."

"Gabby didn't mention that to me. What are the two women's names? I need to call them in for interviews," the sheriff said, grabbing a pen.

"One is Brenda Mann. She graduated from Cupston a year behind me. The other woman is Stephanie, but I don't know her last name. She's from Moosehead," Sage replied.

"I did receive a phone call from Brenda Mann requesting a police escort. She needs to go to the salon and recover her supplies and personal belongings and is afraid of the bodyguard Madame Hand employs."

"He is a big man and extremely scary. He doesn't say much, he just stares at you with those coal-black eyes."

"You had a run-in with him?"

"I did. I got caught nosing around in the back room, and he escorted me out of the building. He's not someone I would want to tangle with."

"We are serving a search warrant on the salon in town this afternoon as soon as the judge signs it. And no, you can't be there," the sheriff said. "Maybe I'll put in a call to Ms. Mann and have her meet us there so she can get her belongings out of the building at the same time."

"Make sure you check out the back room really well," Sage said, standing up. "I'm going to visit Gabby now and make sure she's okay."

"Everything you have seen or heard here in the office has to remain a secret. I admire your common sense, value your input, and trust you explicitly. Don't even discuss it with Gabby since she's still on the suspect list."

"I didn't see or hear anything the whole time I was here visiting with you," Sage said, smiling. "Good luck with the search."

As Sage surmised, the salon was closed. She drove past the building and pulled up in front of Gabby's house. Her friend was out on her porch watering her hanging flowers. She smiled at Sage as she exited her car.

"At least you're still smiling," Sage said, hugging her best friend.

"I'm trying, but it's a real nightmare," Gabby said, setting down her watering can. "Do you want a cup of coffee?"

"I would love a cup."

"Wait here, and I'll bring it out."

The two friends settled in at the patio set with

their coffee. Sage could tell Gabby was exhausted and hadn't slept the night before by the dark circles under her eyes. After several minutes of silence between them, Gabby finally spoke.

"I didn't kill Madame Hand," she blurted out. "I didn't!"

"I know you didn't."

"You may be the only one who thinks so. You and Rory that is."

"The sheriff doesn't, and that's what's important," Sage replied.

"Rory said he told him the back door had been tampered with, but I wasn't to tell anyone," Gabby said.

"Rory told Cliff and me the same thing, but I think he knew he could trust us not to say anything to anyone. Is it true Madame Hand came to your salon yesterday and told you off for stealing her employees?"

"Yes, the lunatic came through the front door screaming and waving her hands around wildly. Half the time, I couldn't even understand what she was saying, and I couldn't get a word in edgewise to shut her up. She scared the daylights out of my poor customers."

"When did you have the chance to threaten her?"

"She stopped screaming long enough to try to catch her breath and I got in her face and demanded she leave. As I escorted her to the door, I told her if she didn't stop bad-mouthing me around town, I would see to it she was permanently stopped from ever doing it again. I meant by filing charges of slander and defamation against her, not killing her."

"Rory told us he was trying to find an attorney for you," Sage replied.

"Now I'm afraid I will need an attorney for a whole different reason," Gabby said, frowning deeply.

"I don't think it will come to that," Sage assured her friend. "Tell me, did you hire Stephanie, too?"

"I did. Thank you for sending Brenda and Stephanie to me. I always wanted to offer those services in my place, if I even have a place after this whole mess is over."

"Did either of them say anything to you about the back room at *To Dye For*?

"Stephanie told me Ricardo guarded the area all day, and no one was allowed in there. If an employee did get caught in there, they were fired. She said one time when she was on her way out at the end of the day, a man came out of the restricted area and held the plastic curtain open as she walked by. She saw the floor had been torn up and there were big holes every-where. When he realized that she was looking inside, he yanked the plastic closed and told her to move on if she knew what was good for her."

"I knew there was something going on that had nothing to do with cutting hair. Excuse me, I have to make a phone call. I'll be right back," Sage said, step-ping down off the porch.

She called Sheriff White to let him know what Gabby had just told her about the floor in the hidden room so he could check it upon his search. He thanked her for the information, and she returned to the porch feeling a little guilty that she was doing things behind her best friend's back; not that she wanted to but out of necessity.

"Everything okay?" Gabby asked.

"Yeah, I just forgot I had to remind Cliff to ask his parents about a price on something I want to purchase from the farm sale donations."

"I get it. You're dating Cliff so you can get special privileges to early viewing and buying," Gabby said, teasing her friend.

"You caught me. No, really, I have a customer request for a six-chair dining set, and all I have are fours in my storage trailer. Cliff mentioned they received an eight-chair set, and I said I would purchase it for the price they would sell it for at the farm sale in the fall. He had to check with his parents on what price to charge for it."

"Sounds like a deal. They get their donation money, and you get a new project to work on that's already sold."

"I know, right? What are you going to do today with the salon closed?"

"Not much. I'm going to stick around the house and do some yard work I've been putting off doing."

"Do you want to go out to lunch? We could go to the diner for one of their famous lunch specials. It would be nice to just sit and talk," Sage suggested.

"I don't know. Word has already circulated around town about me being questioned in the murder. It might get awkward," Gabby said, hesitant about going.

"Locals won't think twice about it. They know the kind of person you are and will know you didn't do it. Come on, what do you say? Lunch?"

"I guess so. Do you want me to pick you up at your place on the way by into town?"

"I'm already going to be there. I have some research to do at the town hall regarding the salon building. I want to look into the history of who owned it in the past and what businesses were previously in there."

"Shall we meet at the diner at one?" Gabby asked.

"Great! That gives me a couple of hours to do my research. See you then," Sage said, walking toward her van.

The town hall was empty with the exception of the employees who worked there. Sage could do her research without prying eyes on her wondering what she was doing. She entered the town clerk's office to sign the book to use the archives in the basement. Waiting for someone to come to the counter to bring her the book, she looked around wondering who had replaced the town clerk, Edna Collins, after she'd been found guilty of murder earlier that year. A familiar face came out of the back room.

"April Topps! Don't tell me you're the new town clerk?" Sage asked, smiling.

"I am. They offered me the job after Edna … well, you know," she replied.

"The selectman couldn't have made a better choice for her replacement. You know this office inside and out. Congratulations!"

"Thanks! I am enjoying the job and the pay raise that went with it," she said, smiling. "What can I do for you today?"

"I need to visit the archives. I'm doing some research to try to help Gabby."

"I heard she was questioned in Madame Hand's murder. I've known Gabby for many years, and there is no way she would ever do anything like murder someone," April said. "She's like a bubble of happiness that floats around bouncing off people, leaving her sunny outlook behind with them."

"That's really nice. Can I tell Gabby what you said? She's kind of down right now."

"Absolutely! Here is the sign-in book. List your name with the date next to it and the last two columns are for check-in and check-out time. I'll leave the book here on the counter for when you leave."

"It was good seeing you again. I can't wait to tell my mom you work here now," Sage said, checking her phone and writing down the time.

"I'm sure my mom has said something to your mom already," April replied. "They have been best friends for a very long time, and I'm sure there are no secrets between them. Can I point you in the direction of where you need to go downstairs?"

"I'm looking for the history of the new salon building. You know… when it was built, it's prior uses and owners, that kind of stuff."

"At the bottom of the stairs turn left and go to the

very back of the room. You should find what you need in that area."

"Thanks, we should go out for lunch sometime," Sage said.

"And Gabby, too," April added as Sage walked out the door toward the basement stairs.

Sage started in the property logs which listed the sales over the previous years and then moved on to newspaper articles of the day. The salon building's address was 134 Old Main Street, and Sage found out the building had been bought and sold many times. The original building was a stand-alone built in 1908. The first owner, Samuel Whittaker, opened a general store, and in 1915, he built an addition to the building which eventually was sold as a separate entity where a barbershop was opened.

Whittaker unexpectedly died in 1920. The general store closed, and his wife moved back to Boston. The building sat vacant for three years until Trentino Hand bought it in 1923.

Now we are getting somewhere. I wonder if Trentino was a distant relative of Ricardo and Madame Hand? It could have something to do with why they wanted to be in the building.

Trentino opened an apothecary which catered to the transient population of gypsies in the area at the time. His wife read palms and crystal balls at the back of the shop. When he opened the upstairs of the building as a flop house, the residents of Cupston rebelled and ran him and his relatives out of town in the middle of the night.

The space sat empty for the next ten years. Apparently, Hand uttered a curse on the property as he rode off that night. No one would buy the property until Daniel Maisy bought the building in 1935. He opened a hardware store and made a good living despite the supposed curse. The building had been passed down through the family and now belonged to Suzanne Maisy.

Since she took possession of it in 1979, she had rented the space out to many different businesses, the last being an artist who used the space as his gallery until he decided to move to Paris. It stayed empty for a couple of months until Madame Hand's new salon opened.

I think the pertinent information here is that Trentino Hand owned the property at one time. Now I have to find out why it was so important for Madame Hand to spend time in the building. I need to pay Ms. Maisy a visit and see what she knows about Trentino Hand.

Sage checked her phone and realized she only had

twenty minutes before she needed to meet Gabby at the diner. She closed the books she'd used and returned them to their correct spaces on the bookshelves. April wasn't around when she returned to the office, so she signed out and left.

Gabby was sitting in her car in the diner parking lot. She looked like she had been crying.

"What's the matter?" Sage asked as her friend rolled down her car window. "What happened?"

"I went inside to wait for you, and I shouldn't have. People were staring, and several made comments that weren't very nice," she replied. "I guess I'm guilty until proven innocent around here."

"Wait here," Sage said.

Claire was behind the register next to the front door.

"Is Gabby all right? I felt so bad for her. Several patrons ganged up on her and weren't very nice," Claire said. "I threw one couple out for what they said and told them not to return to the diner as they wouldn't be welcome here anymore."

"She's in her car crying. After this, I'm afraid she won't come into town anymore until this whole mess has been cleared up," Sage replied. "May I say something to your patrons?"

"Be my guest, just watch the language," Claire said.

"May I have your attention please?" Sage said, walking to the middle of the diner. "To the people who bad-mouthed Gabby Rhodes when she came in here to eat, you ought to be ashamed of yourselves. Gabby has been a law-abiding citizen of this community for many years and is highly thought of by many in Cupston. The garbage that Madame Hand had been dishing out about her was nothing more than trash talk in the hope of stealing Gabby's customers. You're going to look mighty stupid for what you said to her and how you treated her today when the truth comes out and Gabby is found innocent."

Many customers turned and looked at several patrons who had apparently made comments to Gabby. They were fidgeting in their chairs, uncomfortable at the stares they were receiving.

"In this country you are innocent until proven guilty and not the other way around. I just hope the ones in here that are quick to judge never find themselves in the same position Gabby is in right now. You'll owe her a huge apology," Sage said, turning and walking toward the door. "Thank you, Claire, for letting me blow off some steam."

"You tell Gabby she is welcome in here anytime."

"I will, but after today, I don't see her leaving her house much," Sage said. "Have a good day, Claire."

Gabby had left her car and was walking around the parking lot. Sage joined her and offered to buy her a triple decker ice cream cone at *Crazy Cones,* but her friend declined the offer and wanted to go home. She asked Sage what happened inside, and her friend told her what she had done in her defense.

"I have the best friend," Gabby said, hugging her. "I can't believe you did that."

"I did and certain people in Cupston will think twice before they run their mouths in public again," Sage said, laughing.

"I wouldn't have gotten so upset, but the people who spoke up are long-time friends of my parents, and it really hurt they could think I would do something like that."

"Don't worry about them. Maybe they're vying for Edna's position as official town gossip. The town hasn't had a nosy, town gossiper since she left for jail," Sage said, trying to get her friend to smile.

"Too funny," Gabby said. "You may be right."

"I knew I could get you to smile," Sage said. "Why don't you and Rory come over for supper tonight? Cliff will be there. And truthfully, it's not that I don't trust Cliff's ability to screen in the deck, but I would like Rory to look over what he's going to do and see if it's the best and easiest way to enclose the whole area."

"Rory screened in my deck, and I love it, especially during the gnat season."

"How come we don't eat at your house more often then?" Sage asked.

"Because you always say come to my house first," Gabby replied, getting into her car. "See you at six-thirty? I'll bring dessert."

"Sounds good."

Sage watched her best friend drive away and could only imagine what she was feeling.

As sure as my name is Sage Fletcher, I'm going to find out who tried to frame Gabby by putting the body of Madame Hand in her salon.

CHAPTER FOUR

When she first returned home, she took another steak out of her freezer for Gabby and Rory to share. She searched through her pantry for four large potatoes, slathered the skins with butter, salt and pepper and wrapped them in tinfoil to throw on the grill to cook alongside the steaks.

Sage returned to her workshop and worked a few hours before she had to quit for the day and prepare for her company. This coming weekend, she would attend an estate sale in Moosehead, since the newspaper write-up listed many items she would be interested in checking out. It wasn't like she didn't have enough projects now to work on, but her storage trailer was only half full, and she needed to stock up on things she could work on through the cold weather months when there were no yard sales and very few estate sales. She made a mental note to ask Gabby if she wanted to go with her if her salon was still closed.

At six o'clock, Sage threw the potatoes on the grill since they would take longer than the steaks to cook. She made a green salad as a side dish.

I don't know why, but salads taste so much better in the summer.

"Hello! Delivery of farm fresh produce here! Any takers?"

"You must be able to read minds," Sage said, smiling at Cliff who put two paper bags on the kitchen table. "I just used my last tomato in the salad for supper tonight."

"I brought some summer and zucchini squash. Maybe we could have that some night this week? I like the way you prepare it by mashing it up and adding butter and salt and pepper. My mom just slices it, boils it, and puts it on the plate."

"We can do that. Gabby and Rory are joining us for supper."

Sage explained the day's events at the diner and how low her friend was feeling when she left downtown Cupston. She also told Cliff that Rory would be helping him with the plans to screen in the deck. He laughed and told her he'd assumed it would be just like screening in a hen house on the farm, but he would welcome any help from Rory, so it was done the right way.

Smokey and Motorboat were circling Sage's legs and meowing. It was their suppertime, and they wanted food.

"Gabby and Rory should be here any minute. Would you mind throwing the steaks on the grill and turning the potatoes over?" Sage asked. "I have to feed the cats. You'd think they hadn't been fed in days to listen to them."

Cliff went out the slider, and Gabby and Rory came in the front door. Rory grabbed a beer from the fridge and joined Cliff out on the deck.

"Who wants homemade blueberry pie with vanilla ice cream for dessert?' Gabby asked, placing the pie on the table and the ice cream in the freezer.

"Please tell me that is one of Mrs. Jackson's pies! I haven't had one since last summer. She stopped making pies for Thanksgiving when she started to go to Florida for the winter. Last September, I tried to talk her into making me some pies I could freeze and cook for the holidays, but she said her pies were not for freezing, only for eating fresh out of the oven. She's quite the spitfire."

"It is one of hers. I stopped by her house this

afternoon on the way home from town. Florida during the winter seems to be good for her. She was covered in flour and seemed so happy. There had to be at least twenty pies scattered around her kitchen and more in the oven cooking. She's going blueberry picking tomorrow morning. She has more energy than I do," Gabby said.

"Remember when we were little, we would pick blueberries for her, and she paid us twenty-five cents per bucket?"

"And we would ride our bikes to the penny candy store in town and spend it all on candy," Gabby said, laughing. "Now that I'm older and look back, we did a lot of work for twenty-five cents."

"We didn't know any different back then. And besides, we got to eat lots of candy because of Mrs. Jackson," Sage replied.

"Steaks are ready," Cliff yelled from the deck.

"Give me a minute to set the table," Sage yelled back.

Sage lit a citronella candle on each end of the picnic table to chase away the bugs. She and Gabby brought out the sides, dishes, and silverware. Cliff made a fridge run and brought out four beers. The four friends sat down to eat.

There was a light breeze which helped to keep the

bugs at bay. During the meal, the conversation centered around the work needed to be done on Sage's deck. Rory believed there was more than enough screen on the roll Cliff had purchased, and he had some scrap two-inch strapping wood that they could use to make sure the screen was securely held in place.

They were eating their pie and ice cream when a familiar voice reverberated through the house coming from the direction of the front door.

"Anyone here?"

"Out back, Sheriff White," Rory replied.

The sheriff turned the corner and stepped up on the deck.

"May I?" he asked, pointing to an empty space on the picnic bench.

"Have a seat. You don't look so good." Sage asked. "Do you want some pie and coffee?"

"Is that Ida Jackson's blueberry pie?" he asked, inhaling deeply.

"Yes, sir."

"I could use something good in my life today. Pie and coffee, please."

"Am I to assume there is a reason you came out here tonight?" Cliff asked.

"We executed the search on the new salon in town

this morning. Ricardo Hand was nowhere to be found. One of the employees let us in. There was no money in the register, and the poor workers didn't know if they should open the salon or not. I sent them all home."

"Did you find anything in the back room?' Sage asked, returning with the pie and coffee for the sheriff, setting it down in front of him. "I didn't give you any ice cream, did you want some?"

"And hide the wonderful taste of Ida's delicious pie? Never!" he replied, taking a big bite. "I'm afraid I have some bad news."

"For whom?" Cliff asked.

"Gabby, you hired Stephanie Parsons to work in your salon, correct?"

"I did. She's starting as soon as the salon reopens."

"She won't be starting work anytime soon," he replied.

"What happened to Stephanie?" Gabby asked. "Tell me she's not dead?"

"No, she's not dead, but we found her under a pile of plywood in the back room of the salon. She was badly beaten up and unconscious. They took her to Cupston General Hospital."

"No one knew she was there?" Rory asked.

"None of the employees stepped foot in the back room because they were all afraid of Ricardo. I don't know how long she'd been there, but one of the women said she showed up at closing time to collect her pedicure supplies from the back room and was told to come back in an hour when the customers wouldn't see her removing her things."

"Did Ricardo tell her that?" Sage asked.

"No, it was his brother who has been hanging around there for the last few days, according to the employees."

"And neither of them were around this morning?" Sage asked, sitting down. "Do you think they've gone on the run?"

"That would be my guess."

"Great, they're gone, and we still don't know what they were up to. Isn't it weird they would leave without Madame Hand's body?"

"It's still at the county morgue."

"Did you ever find out what she was holding in her hand when she was propped up in front of the mirror?" Sage asked.

"Yes, I did. In one hand, she was holding a pair of reading glasses and in the other hand, some gold coins."

"I researched some gypsy customs. A lot of them

are folklore and myths, but some are actual customs. When they die, they are given things to hold they will be able to use in their afterlife," Sage replied. "I guess Madame Hand's eyesight wasn't great and she needed her glasses."

"Kind of like the Egyptians filling the tombs with items needed after passing," Rory stated.

"And I read when they die, pearls are placed in the nostrils to keep evil spirits from entering the body through the openings. If you check her nose and find pearls up there, there will be a good chance she died in her husband's presence, and he wanted to protect her before moving her to Gabby's salon."

"To each his own, I guess," Gabby said, frowning.

"I'll give the coroner a call first thing in the morning. No, I'll call him right now. He's always there late. Excuse me," he said, stepping down off the deck.

"Anyone want more coffee?" Sage asked. "I'm making a new pot."

"Not me, thank you. I'll never sleep tonight, and I need to be up at five," Cliff replied.

"You hit that one right," the sheriff said, returning to his seat. "Carl found two good-sized pearls in her nostrils. I guess we know who placed the corpse in your salon, Gabby," the sheriff said. "I don't understand why Ricardo would leave his wife's body behind."

"Maybe he thought he sent her spirit off as well as he could and didn't need to bother with the body. I did some research at the town hall. Trentino Hand, Ricardo's great grandfather, owned the building many years ago until he was run out of town by the locals who were upset he was allowing gypsies to live on the second floor of his apothecary. The story goes since he was forced out in the middle of the night, he cursed the building. It sat empty for quite a while until the Maisy family bought it, not believing in the curse."

"The floor in the back room was torn to shreds. I wonder if Ricardo and his brother were looking for something left behind by their relatives," the sheriff said.

"Makes sense. I wonder if they found what they were looking for?" Sage said.

"But why beat up Stephanie and leave her there?" Rory asked.

"Maybe she saw something she shouldn't have seen," Sage replied. "If she went back to the salon to get her personal belongings, she could have witnessed them finding whatever it was they were looking for."

"They probably figured she would be dead before

anyone found her," Cliff added. "Ricardo must not have known Madame Hand gave one of the employees a key."

"I've issued an all-points on Ricardo and his brother. Problem is we don't know what they are driving, and we have no idea where they were heading when they left," the sheriff said.

"They could be anywhere at this point," Gabby said.

"Sheriff, didn't you say Madame Hand was holding some gold coins?"

"I did. She had three gold coins, twenty-dollar pieces I believe. Why?"

"What if Trentino Hand had hidden his fortune underneath the floorboards of the building? He probably didn't trust the banks back then since gypsies were not welcome in many places. Could that have been what the brothers were after?"

"I don't know, but that's a good possibility," the sheriff replied. "The wood floor was completely dismantled, and the dirt underneath had large holes dug in it."

"If she was holding gold coins, one would have to assume they found something. You should call Carl back and see what the dates are on the coins," Sage suggested.

"I'll check with him in the morning. Now, I'm going home before my better half files for a divorce," he said, standing up. "Thank you for the pie. Ida's baking never disappoints. I may have to send the wife over to her house to purchase a couple pies."

"My mom suggested she sell her pies at the farm stand over the summer. Ida is considering it," Cliff said. "If she does, I'll be buying them up and freezing them, but don't tell Ida. She'll throw a hissy fit at the thought of one of her pies being frozen."

"I think quite a few locals around here will do the exact same thing, me included," the sheriff said, chuckling. "I'll be in touch."

"Let me help with the dishes," Gabby offered.

"Just help me bring everything inside, and I will take care of the rest. Watch out for the cats scooting out under your feet. They're quick little boogers when they want to be," Sage said.

The candles were extinguished, and each person took an armload of dishes inside to the kitchen. The cats were nowhere to be found. Sage found them curled up together behind the couch.

"I'll be over on Sunday to work on screening in the deck. Cliff, ten o'clock okay?" Rory asked.

"Sounds good. I'll meet you here."

"It shouldn't take more than a couple of hours," Rory replied.

"I'll supply the beer and lunch," Sage said.

"I promised I'd take my mom to Moosehead on Sunday. She wants to go to the flower show, and it's kind of our thing we do together every year," Gabby said. "Sorry I won't be here, but you're better off without my help anyway. I'm a bang-your-thumb-with-the-hammer kind of person."

"I'll vouch for that," Rory said, smiling at his fiancée. "See you guys Sunday."

"I have to be in Boston for the next two days for a tractor show. I'll be back late Saturday night, but I won't see you until Sunday," Cliff said as they walked to the driveway. "Try to stay out of trouble while I'm gone."

"I'll be right here working in my shop, and on Saturday, I'm going to yard sales and to an estate sale in Moosehead. How can I get into trouble with that schedule?" she asked, smiling.

"You'll find a way," he said, giving her a quick kiss on the cheek.

"Have a great trip," Sage said, waving as Cliff pulled out of her driveway.

"Come on, guys, let's clean up the kitchen," she said to the cats who were sitting at the door waiting for her to return. "There might even be a scrap or two of steak for you."

She cut up what remained of her piece of steak from supper and divided it on two plates.

"Now, each of you stick to your own plate," she said, setting them down on the floor.

The cats finished before Sage had even finished loading the dishwasher. They disappeared into the living room and up into the bay window to clean themselves. She shut off the kitchen light and went to her bedroom to get in her pajamas.

Sitting on one end of the couch, she turned on the light on the end table. She had bought a new historical mystery set in London during WWII that she had been dying to start. As hard as she tried, she couldn't concentrate on reading.

The cats had joined her and were curled up next to her legs.

Great, my computer is across the room, and if I get up, I'll disturb the cats. Maybe it's a sign I should just go to bed. I have to remember to call Mrs. Maisy in the morning to see if I can visit with her.

"So much for reading. Come on boys, it's time for bed."

The next morning, Sage was on her way to Miss Maisy's house by nine o'clock. When she placed her call earlier in the morning, the elderly woman said she was happy to meet with her and have some company for tea. Her house was located on the outskirts of town and had a long winding driveway.

A small Cape, painted in white with black shutters was at the end of the driveway. A freshly painted white picket fence enclosed the front yard. A sea of color surrounded the house due to a large variety of flowers planted everywhere. Sage exited her car and took a deep breath. The smell was exhilarating.

"Isn't it wonderful?" Miss Maisy asked from her doorway. "The smell I mean. I sit out here during the day watching the bees buzzing around, collecting their pollen and my beautiful flowers swaying in the soft breezes."

"I would be out here all day too if I lived here," Sage said.

"Would you like to have tea on the patio?"

"That would be wonderful," Sage said, smiling.

They entered the cottage heading for the kitchen. The place was exactly how Sage had imagined it would be when standing outside. Dainty handmade doilies adorned the furniture, and collectible images were on display throughout the house. One statue in particular caught her eye. A gypsy woman, with her hands poised gracefully above her head, displayed in a twirling motion as if dancing was sitting on a table in the far corner of the room.

"Isn't she stunning?" Miss Maisy asked, walking up to Sage.

"She is. Does your family have gypsy lineage, if you don't mind me asking?"

"Oh, no, my dear. I found that beauty many years ago when I first inherited the shop in town from my father. I was remodeling the inside of the place to rent it and found this below the rotted floorboards. It was buried in the dirt with only the hands exposed."

"May I?" Sage asked, motioning to the figurine.

"Yes. There goes the teakettle. I'll be back with our tea in a moment."

Sage carefully picked up the statue. She had a gut feeling this must have belonged to Trentino Hand. What was so special about it that it had to be buried for safekeeping? She turned it over perusing the bottom. Made in Romania was stamped on the bottom in gold letters with a handwritten name underneath it that Sage could not make out.

Miss Maisy returned with the tray of tea and cookies ready to go out to the patio.

"May I bring this with us?" Sage requested.

"Yes, but please be careful with it."

Sage opened the door for her hostess. She set the

statue in the center of the patio table so it would not fall and break. Miss Maisy poured the tea, all the time smiling, and then offered Sage a small plate with cookies on it.

"Am I right to assume you are here to ask about Trentino Hand?"

"I am and to ask about the history of the building you own. I did some research on it, but I was hoping you could fill in some of the holes."

"What do you want to know?"

"When your dad gave you the building, you said you did a remodel on the inside of the space. Did you find anything else besides the dancing gypsy buried in the dirt, Miss Maisy?"

"Suzanne, please. As a matter of fact, I did. How did you know?"

"I believe the Hands rented the space looking for what was buried underneath the building. They had no intention of running a business there but had to have a cover story for what they were doing there. What else did you find?"

"I found five coins, all twenty-dollar gold pieces. I still have them around here somewhere."

"I am sure they are worth a decent amount of money in today's market, but it hardly seems like an amount they would almost kill someone for," Sage said. "Unless they thought there were many more coins buried there."

"I did find one other item but not buried in the dirt. It was hidden in the wall."

"Something tied to Trentino Hand?"

"Yes, it was a daily journal penned by his wife, Margo. Judging from the entries, she must have kept the book hidden from her husband since she doesn't speak favorably about him at all. I think she was quite afraid of him actually."

"Have you read the whole journal?" Sage asked while looking over the statue again.

"No, I only read about halfway through before I decided to hide it. Back in the seventies when I found it, gypsies were still stigmatized with the reputation of being liars and thieves and placing curses on people and places. Of course, like with anything, there were some who lived up to the reputation, but on the whole, most did not. The building's history of being cursed had been pretty much forgotten. I wanted to rent the place and didn't want the curse to resurface again."

"Do you still have the journal?"

"It's up in the attic in an old trunk in the far corner. Would you like to read it?" the elderly woman asked.

"I sure would," Sage said, almost jumping out of her chair.

"Follow me. I'll show you where the attic stairs are located."

Suzanne turned on the light, and Sage started up the stairs by herself.

"Look for a sea trunk in the far-right corner of the room. You may have to move some things to get to it because I haven't been near it in years," Suzanne yelled up the stairs. "The journal will be at the bottom of the trunk since I wanted to keep it hidden."

"Found it," yelled Sage.

The two women returned to the patio.

"This is amazing. You took very good care of it. The words are still legible throughout most of the book," Sage said, carefully flipping the pages. "May I take this home with me tonight to read it?"

Yes, but please don't tell anyone you have it."

"It will be our secret, I promise. I know this is a lot to ask, but may I take the dancing gypsy with me also? I'd like to examine it more closely with my magnifying glass."

"Why the interest in the statue?" Suzanne asked, sipping her now cold tea.

"This must have been important to Trentino's wife for her to bury it under the floorboards. The clue to why might be in the journal. I will keep everything secret because if word did get out that you had these items, Ricardo and his brother might come looking for them," Sage replied. "They beat a friend of mine almost to death at the salon. They are dangerous men, and whatever they are looking for must be really important to them."

"I saw the damage they did to the back room of my building. Thank goodness for insurance. They were definitely looking for something under the building, and the sheriff told me that Madame Hand died of an aneurism."

"She did, and we think Ricardo put her in Gabby's salon to try to frame her for murder."

"Ricardo, really?"

"Yes, there were pearls up the nostrils of Madame Hand which is a custom followed to keep the evil spirits out of the body. We think he protected his wife and then left her at Gabby's place."

"He left the body behind?"

"Yes. Does that mean something to you?"

"When I was a little girl, my dad would tell me stories about the gypsies or Wanderers as some people called them. He told me of ritualistic ceremonies that were celebrated when a gypsy died. They would return the body to where they considered home. On the day of the funeral, they would parade the body past landmarks that meant something to the dead person, stopping so the deceased could connect with those places before they arrived at the cemetery for their final burial. It seems odd that her husband would leave the body behind and not honor her in that way. Then again, that was years ago, and things may have changed."

"Do you think they will try to take the body back?" Sage asked.

"I don't know, could be."

"Madame Hand's body is being held at the county morgue. Do you think they will break in and take her home?"

"Like I said, I don't know how much the old customs have changed in the present day," Suzanne said. "I would tell Sheriff White to watch the place a little more closely at night."

"I want to thank you for seeing me today and trusting me with your personal possessions," Sage said, standing up to leave. "I will pass on your message to the sheriff. If I learn anything important from the journal or the statue, I will contact you immediately."

"Let me get you a box to protect my porcelain dancer."

Once in the car, she called the sheriff's office to pass on Suzanne's story about the funeral custom. He was out on a call, but Deputy Barr promised to pass on her message. At home, Sage poured herself a glass of wine and sat at the kitchen table to start reading the journal. The box containing the statue had been hidden in her bedroom closet for safety reasons.

The journal covered a span of six years. The entries were written sporadically and not every day. It was obvious that Margo was afraid of her husband. She had been sold to him at age sixteen in an arranged marriage by her own father. He was twenty-four years older than she was, and her sole responsibility was to bear children to carry on the Hand line.

They left Romania and settled in a small community named Pascale, just north of what is now Portland, Maine. Margo was happy there. She had many friends and gave birth to three children. Some years later, Trentino came into a large sum of money, from where Margo did not know, and he purchased the building in Cupston where he became a feared leader of the gypsy community.

Margo wrote that the more people who followed her husband, the more dangerous and cruel he became. Many days, she hid in her room to avoid the everyday trials that were held in the apothecary. Trials of people who dared to speak up against her husband's will and wants.

Trentino became one of the most powerful gypsies in the Northeastern region. But his wife knew the secret to his power. A power that had been granted to him from another gypsy king from Romania. It was the ring. A blood ruby ring that when people saw it on his finger, they cowered in his presence. The ring, the Gypsy King ring, meant he was a chosen one and should be revered.

Many of Margo's entries named people who had come to trial and then were never seen again. She never knew if her husband was a murderer or had others do his bidding. The one thing she did know was now that she had borne him five children, three of which were sons, her time was limited. She was not needed anymore. As the crowned Gypsy King here in America, the women worshiped him, all women.

Margo wrote in a very detailed entry of what she knew she had to do. She had to get the ring and hide it where her husband could not find it. At least then if she died, she knew she would leave behind a weaker man and possibly destroy him altogether. Without the ring, he would be nothing.

I wonder if it was the ring Ricardo was looking

for. Maybe he knew of its status and power and wanted to follow in his great grandfather's footsteps.

The next entry told the story of how Margo waited until her husband was drunk from drinking whiskey with his closest friends. He passed out at the table where he sat. Patiently waiting for the rest of the drinkers to either stumble away or pass out, she took the ring off his finger. He never moved.

Taking the ring to the first floor, she took the dancing gypsy her mother had given to her before she left Romania and softly hit the bottom with a jeweler's hammer. A hole opened wide enough that she could squeeze the ring into the bottom of the statue. Taking strips of white cloth, she cut them to cover the hole and applied a thin coat of white plaster to the cloth to seal it closed.

Prying up a floorboard, she buried the statue in the dirt below leaving only the outstretched hands showing. This was her symbol of freedom and the end of a tyrant. Sage dropped the journal on the table and ran to retrieve the statue from her closet.

"I knew the bottom was uneven," she said to Smokey who had jumped up on the chair next to her and was pawing at the edge of the box. "No, you can't get in there. It doesn't belong to us."

I can see the patch, but I can't open it without Suzanne's permission.

She placed a call to her new friend and told her what she had discovered hidden in the entries of the journal. The elderly woman gave her permission to open the statue. Sage kept her on speaker while she tried to break through the patched hole. The plaster, being over a hundred years old, crumbled at the first hit.

"I'm in," Sage said to Suzanne.

"I can't believe all these years I never knew it was there. I guess I should have read the journal all the way through," Suzanne said through the phone.

Sage reached her finger in the hole and felt around. She felt a cold, smooth, round item which seemed to be stuck on the inside of what was left of the plaster patch. Wiggling it, the ring finally fell through the hole.

"I have it," she said to Suzanne. "It's stunning."

The ring itself was made of gold. There was a huge blood ruby set in the center of the ring. On either side of the ruby were inlaid diamonds, one forming a cross and one forming a dagger.

"You had it," a man's voice said behind her.

Sage whirled around to see two men standing just inside her slider door.

"Ricardo! What are you doing here? Get out of my house," Sage demanded of the men.

"Not without the ring."

"How did you know I had it?" Sage asked, shoving the ring in her jean pocket and hoping Suzanne had still been listening and would call the sheriff.

"We have been looking for the gypsy dancer since the first day we rented my great-grandfather's building. On her deathbed, my great-grandmother told her best friend where she had hidden the ring. She told my grandfather, and the story has been passed down through the men in the family. The only problem was we didn't know which building it was hidden in as Trentino owned quite a few in Maine at the height of his power."

"So you went from building to building pulling up the floors looking for the statue?"

"We did. It was my son who figured out the end of the story and what building it was in. Trentino lived in Cupston when he lost his power, and they ran him out of town. The ring had to have been taken from him here, so we rented the building and started looking, not figuring that the owner had found it years ago."

"But how did you know the dancing gypsy was

here with me?" Sage asked, pushing the ring deeper into her pocket.

"We watched the old lady's house. We waited for her to leave so we could break in and steal the statue, but she never went anywhere. Then we saw you take the statue with you, so we followed you here."

"I hope you don't think you will get away with this. You hurt our friend Stephanie. She's in the hospital, still in a coma."

"She's lucky she's not dead and we let her live. Women should do as they're told, and she was told to stay out of the back room. She didn't listen, and she overheard us discussing the ring when she returned for her things. I really thought by the time anyone found her, she would be dead. It doesn't matter, we'll be long gone before she wakes up, if she even does," he said, laughing.

"You're just like your great-grandfather. A miserable excuse for a human being," Sage said. "No regard for human life as long as you get what you want."

"You watch what you say about my family," Ricardo snarled, taking a knife out of his belt and advancing toward her. "Now, are you going to give me the ring, or do I have to take it?"

"Do you seriously believe that a ring, an inanimate object, can give you power?" Sage asked, stalling for time.

"You do not understand my culture, or you would not ask. That ring is a gypsy king's ring from Romania. Whoever wears it holds all the power and the luck of the gypsies. Whoever wears it becomes the Gypsy King and is revered. I am the rightful heir as the oldest son of my deceased father."

"What about Madame Hand? Was she just a means to get what you wanted that you could throw her away like you did?"

"I have not thrown her away as you say. We will be taking her body tonight and returning her to her home she loved, and then I will return to my beloved Romania as a new king. Now, give me the ring."

As Ricardo advanced, he spotted the cell phone on the table. He picked it up, and when the screen lit up, he saw there was someone on the other end.

"Who was listening?" he asked, demanding to know, shutting off the phone and smashing it on the floor.

"I guess you'll never know now that you smashed my phone," she replied.

That was the last thing Sage remembered saying as she felt a blow to the side of her head and fell to the floor.

CHAPTER FIVE

"Sage, wake up," Sheriff White said, kneeling next to her. "Talk to me. Why is the ambulance taking so long to get here?"

Sage moaned and put her hand to her head. Her eyes fluttered open to see a concerned sheriff's face looking down on her. She grabbed for her jean pocket looking for the ring. Instead, she found that her pocket had been cut open and the ring was gone.

"He got the ring," she mumbled. "Where are my cats? Are they okay?"

"What ring? Suzanne mentioned a ring also. Your cats are locked in the den and are fine."

Sage's mother came flying in through the front door with a loud bang.

"Where is my daughter?" she said, coming into the kitchen. "Sage, oh sweetie."

"How did you find out so fast?" the sheriff asked.

"Suzanne called me after she called you. I closed the shop and came right over," Sarah answered. "Have you called an ambulance? My daughter needs to go to the hospital to be checked out."

"It's on its way."

"He's going to get the body. Tonight," Sage said, struggling to get the words out. "He's probably already there."

"Don't you worry. We have the place staked out and will be ready for them if and when they show up."

"You have to get him. He's leaving for Romania as soon as he buries his wife."

"We'll get him. You just rest and quit talking. The ambulance is on the way," the sheriff said. "Sarah, stay with Sage. I have to go call my men and tell them to be ready for Ricardo's arrival if he's not already there."

"He has … a knife, a big knife. Tell them … to be careful," Sage said, catching her breath between words.

With that warning issued, she closed her eyes and lost consciousness.

The next morning, Sage woke up in a hospital bed with her mother, Cliff, and Gabby sitting by her bedside. She smiled knowing she was safe surrounded by all those who loved her.

"I thought I told you to stay out of trouble while I was gone," Cliff said, joking with her to break the tension in the room.

"I did. I was in my house, minding my own business. Can I help it if trouble followed me home? And what are you even doing here?"

"You don't seriously think I am going to stay at some old tractor show when something has happened to my girlfriend, do you? Gabby called me, and I came right home."

A smile broke across Sarah's face when Cliff called her daughter his girlfriend.

The doctor knocked on the door and entered the room. After looking over her charts, he told her she could go home later that afternoon, but she had to promise to take it easy for a few days. There was no permanent damage done but she would probably have a headache that would stick around for twenty-four to forty-eight hours and if she had any dizzy spells, she should return to the hospital immediately.

Sage's breakfast was delivered. As she ate, it was decided that Sarah and Gabby would run home and shower and change into clean clothes and meet back at her house when she was released. Cliff would stay with Sage and give her a ride home.

"I'm so glad you're all right," Sarah said, tearing up as she hugged her daughter. "I don't know what I would have done if anything happened to you."

"Everything's going to be fine, Mom. Why don't you go open your shop and plan to meet at my house for dinner?"

"Are you sure? The shop doesn't have to open today. I'm sure people would understand if it was closed."

"I'm sure. Go to work and don't worry. I have my boyfriend here to watch over me," she said, watching Cliff's face for a reaction.

He looked at Sage and smiled. She thought for a split second, she could see his chest puff up like he was having a proud moment.

"I'll take good care of her," he replied, reaching for Sage's hand.

"You'd better or you'll answer to me, young man," Sarah said, walking out the door and blowing a kiss to her daughter.

"I need to call Rory to tell him you'll be okay," Gabby said, standing up and pushing her chair back in the corner. "Let's all meet at your house tonight so you can fill us in on what happened. Don't you dare get off your couch this afternoon. I'll bring supper and dessert for everyone."

"Sounds awesome. I guess this means you are in the clear now, doesn't it? Those people at the diner are going to feel pretty foolish now that they ran their mouths the way they did."

"It doesn't really matter what they said anymore. My real friends, my true friends stuck by me, and that's all that matters to me. The sheriff did call me last night saying I could reopen the salon whenever I wanted to. I told him I was going to take the weekend to pull everything together and open next Monday."

"And you will have two new services to offer your clients when you do open," Sage added.

"One for right now. Stephanie is not out of the woods yet, but she is improving according to the doctors. Her mom and dad are here from Moosehead staying with her. I talked to them this morning when I was checking on her condition. They offered to find their daughter somewhere to live in Cupston if the job was still available. I assured them it was, and they said they would get to work finding a rental for her so she wouldn't have to travel to and from Moosehead every day."

"All good news. Now if I could just hear from the

sheriff with news about whether or not they caught Ricardo and his brother, my day would be complete."

"You will, I'm sure," Gabby said. "I'll see you at six thirty."

"Do you mind if I rest a little? I don't want to be rude not talking to you while you are here," Sage asked.

"You rest. I'll go to the cafeteria and get some breakfast," he replied, leaning over and kissing the bandage on her head.

"Cliff, thanks for being here."

"I wouldn't be anywhere else at this moment," he said, heading for the door. "Rest now."

Sage and Cliff spent the day together once she was released from the hospital. She lay in the hammock while Cliff did the prep work for screening in the deck. At six o'clock, Sage's mother showed up at the house carrying a big bowl of potato salad and a bottle of wine. Minutes later, Gabby and Rory pulled in.

Gabby got busy in the kitchen and asked Cliff to turn on the grill so it would warm up to cook the steaks and shrimp that she had brought with her for supper.

"You have enough food to feed an army," Sage said, joking with her friend.

"Oh, I might have forgotten to tell you when I called earlier to ask how much beer was in the fridge. I ran into Sheriff White on the way out of the hospital and invited him and his wife to have supper with us. I hope that's okay," Gabby replied.

"That's awesome. It will be nice to finally meet his wife."

"And he has some news to tell you," Gabby said, smiling.

"He caught Ricardo, didn't he?" Sage asked.

"You'll have to wait for the sheriff to get here," Gabby said, teasing her friend.

Everyone was out on the deck when the sheriff and his wife arrived.

"This is my wife, Ella," he announced and proceeded to introduce each person there.

"Oh, Ella and I know each other," Sarah said, giving her friend a hug. "We go way back."

"Sheriff, would you like a beer? Ella, beer, wine, water, or a soda?" Sage asked.

"I would love a glass of wine," she answered. "Can I help with anything?"

"If you want to help carry out some of the food to the table, that would be great. Our patient is supposed to be taking it easy," Gabby replied. "Unfortunately, she doesn't listen very well."

"I listen. How strenuous is it to get someone a glass of wine? Geez!" Sage said, rolling her eyes.

A short time later, they were all seated around the picnic table filling their plates with delicious food. Sage tried to be patient, not asking about whether or not they caught the brothers. Finally, she couldn't wait any longer and blurted out her question to the sheriff. Everyone broke out laughing with the exception of Ella who didn't get what was so funny.

"I bet you've been waiting all day to ask that question, haven't you?" the sheriff asked, chuckling. "What took you so long to ask me?"

"I was trying not to be rude. Well, are you going to catch me up on what happened at the coroner's office or not?"

"I won't keep you in suspense any longer. Ricardo and his brother arrived at the morgue and parked around the back of the building. What they didn't know was my men and the state police were hiding in the vans and hearses parked in the lot."

"Did they get them?" Sage asked again.

"Hold on. They watched as the brothers tried to jimmy the back door, and when they were so involved in what they were doing, the men jumped out of their hiding places and closed in. Ricardo attempted to pull his knife on the officers which added another several charges to the list that already existed."

"He was wrestled to the ground and cuffed. The brother gave up rather easily."

"Did you recover the ring?" Sage asked.

"We did. He blew up when we took the ring out of his car. He started screaming in some language which we assume was Romanian. Then in English he cursed us all and all our family members."

"Just like his great-grandfather did in Cupston over a hundred years ago," Sage replied. "What will happen to the ring?"

"It will be returned to Miss Maisy. I don't know if she'll want it or not, and if she doesn't, she can sell it to cover the cost of repairing her building. How did you know about the ring in the first place?" the sheriff asked.

"I went to visit Miss Maisy to ask about the history of the building. We started talking, and she told me about a journal she found hidden in the wall of the building back in the seventies when she was remodeling. The journal was written by Trentino's wife. She was afraid of her husband and the power of the ring. She stole it off his finger one night when he was drunk and passed out. She also wrote about what she did with the ring so he would never find it again.

She sealed it in the statue of the dancing gypsy and buried it under the floorboards at the apothecary."

"How did Ricardo find out about the location of the ring?" Gabby asked.

"On her death bed, she confided in a close friend where she hid the ring. And of course the friend went right to Ricardo's grandfather and told him what was said. Ricardo said the story had been passed down by the men in the family. He felt he was the rightful heir to be Gypsy King and wear the ring, and he came looking for it."

"Gypsy King or not, he's looking at many years in prison. There are eleven pending charges against him here, and when we pulled up his name in the system, we discovered he's the top suspect in a brutal murder in Portland from four years ago. He will never return to Romania again," the sheriff replied.

"Gabby, are you going to be opening your salon anytime soon?" Ella asked. "I could use a haircut and perm."

"We'll be reopening on Monday."

"And my nails could use some attention. My husband tells me you are about to become a full-service salon. That's exciting."

"I am. As soon as Stephanie recovers, she will be joining us at the salon."

"There goes all my money," the sheriff groaned.

"Do you want a beautiful wife or not?" she asked, elbowing her husband in the ribs.

"You're beautiful even if you don't go to the salon," the sheriff replied.

"Is this what married life is like?" Rory asked, smiling. "At least my wife will be the stylist, and I won't have to pay for all those services."

"Don't think you'll be getting off that easy, Rory Nash," Gabby said, smiling.

"Duly noted," he replied.

"Anyone need a refill on their drinks?" Sage asked, standing up.

Almost everyone needed a refill, and Cliff offered to go to the kitchen with her to help. As Sage poured the wine into Ella's glass, Cliff wrapped his arms around her waist from behind.

"As the person with the new title of boyfriend, I have to ask."

"Ask away," Sage said.

"Is your life always this hectic? Us good old farm boys aren't used to all this excitement."

She turned around to face him.

"Well, if this farm boy is going to be sticking around, he better get used to it. My life has been like this since I was young, and truthfully, I wouldn't want it to be any different than it is."

"Oh, I'm going to be sticking around for a long time to come," he said, kissing her.

"Hey, where's my beer?" Rory yelled from the deck.

"Our friends are thirsty." Sage laughed, picking up the two wine glasses. "You got the beers?"

"I do," he answered, leading the way to the door.

Sage hoped that it would be a few years before Cliff said those words again.

Printed in Great Britain
by Amazon